Sheep in a Jeep

5-minute stories

written by **Nancy Shaw**

illustrated by **Margot Apple**

Houghton Mifflin Harcourt

Boston   New York

For information about permission to
reproduce selections from this book, write
to trade.permissions@hmhco.com or to
Permissions, Houghton Mifflin Harcourt
Publishing Company, 3 Park Avenue,
19th Floor, New York, New York 10016.

hmhco.com

JEEP ® is a registered trademark of Chrysler Corporation.

ISBN: 978-1-328-56674-4

Manufactured in China
SCP 10 9 8 7 6 5 4 3 2 1
4500743724

Contents

Sheep in a Jeep

Beep! Beep!
Sheep in a jeep
on a hill that's
steep.

Uh-oh!
The jeep won't go.

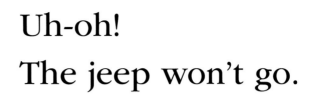

Sheep leap
to push the jeep.

Sheep shove.
Sheep grunt.

Sheep don't think
to look up front.

Jeep goes splash!
Jeep goes thud!

Jeep goes deep
in gooey mud.

Sheep tug.

Sheep shrug.

Sheep yelp.

Sheep get help.

Jeep comes out.

Sheep shout.

Sheep cheer.

Oh, dear!
The driver sheep
forgets to steer.

Jeep in a heap.

Sheep weep.

Sheep sweep
the heap.

Jeep for sale — cheap.

Sheep Trick or Treat

As the Halloween moon rises,
sheep are fixing up disguises.

They make a mask with glue and tape
and a monster suit with a shiny cape.

Sheep snip and sew and drape
a costume for a giant ape.

Sheep shape wool in pointy clumps
to make a dinosaur with bumps.

Sheep rip scraps for mummy wraps.

Sheep pose in spooky clothes.

Sheep take lanterns. Arm in arm,
they set off for a nearby farm.

In the woods, they give three cheers.
A sleepy wolf perks up his ears.

Sheep amble to the dell.
They reach the barn and ring the bell.

Sheep bleat. Trick or treat!

Animals give them things to eat.
The horses' treats go in with thumps:
apples, oats, and sugar lumps.

Spiders give a dried-up fly.

Sheep decide to pass it by.

Sheep stop by the chicken coops.

Chickens give them fresh eggs. Oops!

Cows offer hay and clover.

Now the trick-or-treating's over.

Back through the woods
the sheep parade.

It's dark, but they are not afraid.

Rustling noises come from trees.

Is someone there, or just a breeze?

Wolves peek out from hiding places.

The Dell

Wolves see scary lit-up faces.

Wolves skedaddle.

Sheep skip past.

They settle down with treats at last.

Sheep in a Shop

A birthday's coming! Hip hooray!

Five sheep shop for the big, big day.

Sheep find rackets. Sheep find rockets.

Sheep find jackets full of pockets.

Sheep find blocks.
Sheep wind clocks.

Sheep try trains. Sheep fly planes.

Sheep decide to buy a beach ball.
Sheep prefer an out-of-reach ball.

Sheep climb. Sheep grumble.
Sheep reach. Sheep fumble.

Sheep sprawl.
Boxes tumble.

Boxes fall in one big jumble.

Sheep put back the beach ball stack. They choose some ribbon from the rack.

They dump their bank. Pennies clank.

There's not enough to buy this stuff.

Sheep blink. Sheep think.

What can they swap to pay the shop?

Sheep clip wool, three bags full.

Sheep trade.

The bill is paid.

Sheep hop home in the warm spring sun.

They're ready for some birthday fun.

Sheep Take a Hike

Morning's here! It's warm and clear!

Sheep load up their hiking gear.

Compass, whistles, drinks, and snacks go in packs upon their backs.

They trot along a hiking trail

up the hill and down the dale.

Trees and bushes soon grow thicker.
Where's the trail? Sheep bicker.

Sheep squeeze through the trees.
Sheep rush through underbrush.

Thorns dig. Prickers snag.
Sheep zig. Sheep zag.

Fog comes up. The ground feels damp.

On and on, sheep tramp.

Sheep stomp into a swamp.
Moosh! Goosh! Boggy tracks!

Yuck! Muck! Soggy backs!
Blub! Blub! Sloppy packs!
Glub! Glub! Gloppy snacks!

The compass sinks. They're in dismay.
How can they ever find their way?

Sheep climb out of the slime.

They look around, and soon they find

woolly fuzz they left behind.

Sheep won't stray—
they've marked the way!

Now they're on the hiking path.

What more could they want . . . a bath!

Sheep trot homeward. Rain pours.

What a day for the great outdoors!

Sheep Blast Off!

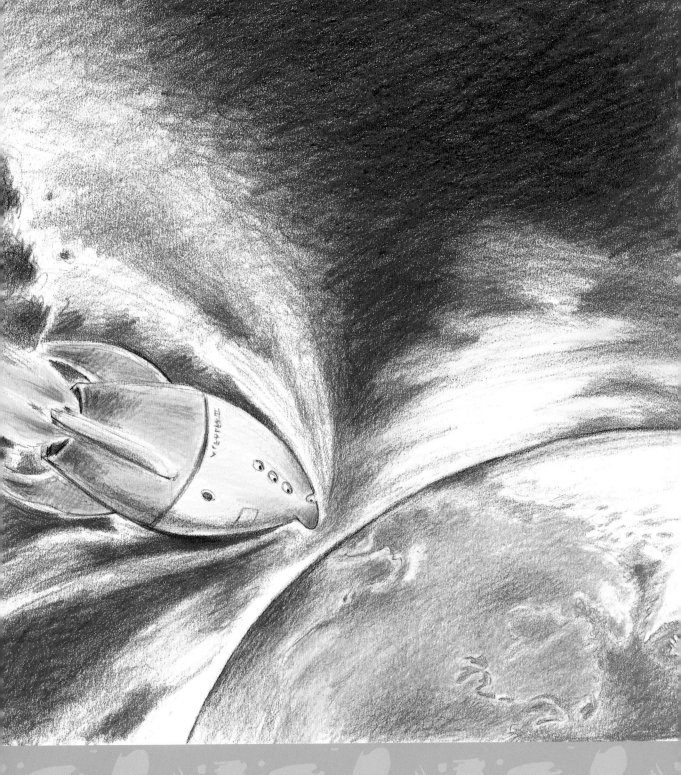

Sheep see a shape in the mist, by a tree.

Something has landed! What can it be?

Sheep snoop. Sheep explore.

Sheep climb through the spaceship door.

Sheep stumble. Sheep bumble.
Engines slowly start to rumble.

They grab a knob. It seals the door.
Lights come on. Engines roar.

Everyone gets into gear.
They blast right through
the stratosphere.

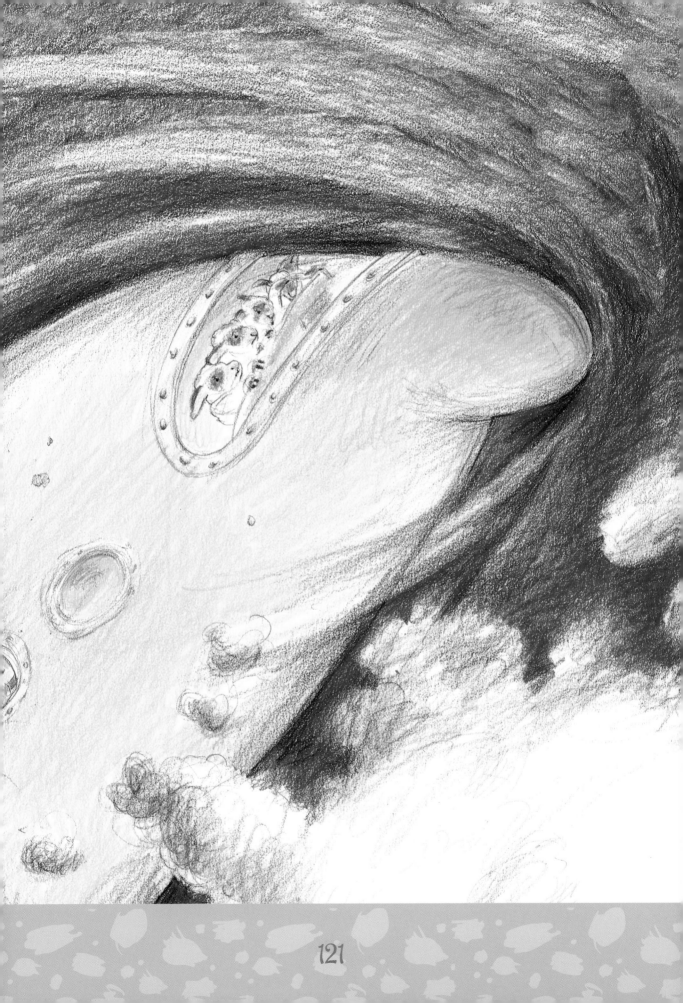

Around the world
the rocket zips.
Weightless sheep
do jumps and flips.

What's that thump? They hit the deck.

Two sheep float
outside to check.

There's just a scratch.
It looks okay.

Back through the hatch—
they're on their way.

They tinker with the main controls.
The rocket lurches, swoops, and rolls.

Lights flash.
Computers beep.

Blaring sirens scare the sheep.

Sheep panic. Sheep guess.
Which button should they press?

Autopilot! That's the one!

Leaving orbit! Nicely done!

Prepare for touchdown!

Home at last!

Rocket sheep have had a blast.

Sheep Out to Eat

Five sheep stop at a small teashop.

They ask for a seat
and a bite to eat.

Sheep get menus. Sheep want feed.

They point to words that they can't read.

Sheep get soup. Sheep scoop.

Sheep slurp. Sheep burp.

Waiters bring them spinach custard.
Sheep add sugar, salt, and mustard.

Sheep take a few bites.
Sheep lose their appetites.

Waiters bring them tea and cake.

Sheep add pepper by mistake.

Sheep chomp. Sheep sneeze.

Sheep jump and bump their knees.

Table tips. Teacups smash.

Tea drips. Dishes crash.

Dishes break. Waiters stare.

Tea and cake are everywhere.

Waiters mop all the slop.

They ask the sheep to leave the shop.

Sheep pout. Sheep walk out.

Suddenly they look about.

Sheep crunch. Sheep munch.

The lawn is what they want for lunch.

Sheep smack lips. Sheep leave tips.

They'll stop again on other trips.

Sheep on a Ship

Sheep sail
a ship
on a
deep-sea
trip.

Waves lap.
Sails flap.

Sheep read a map

but begin to nap.

Dark clouds form
a sudden storm.

It rains and hails
and shakes the sails.

Sheep wake up
and grab the rails.

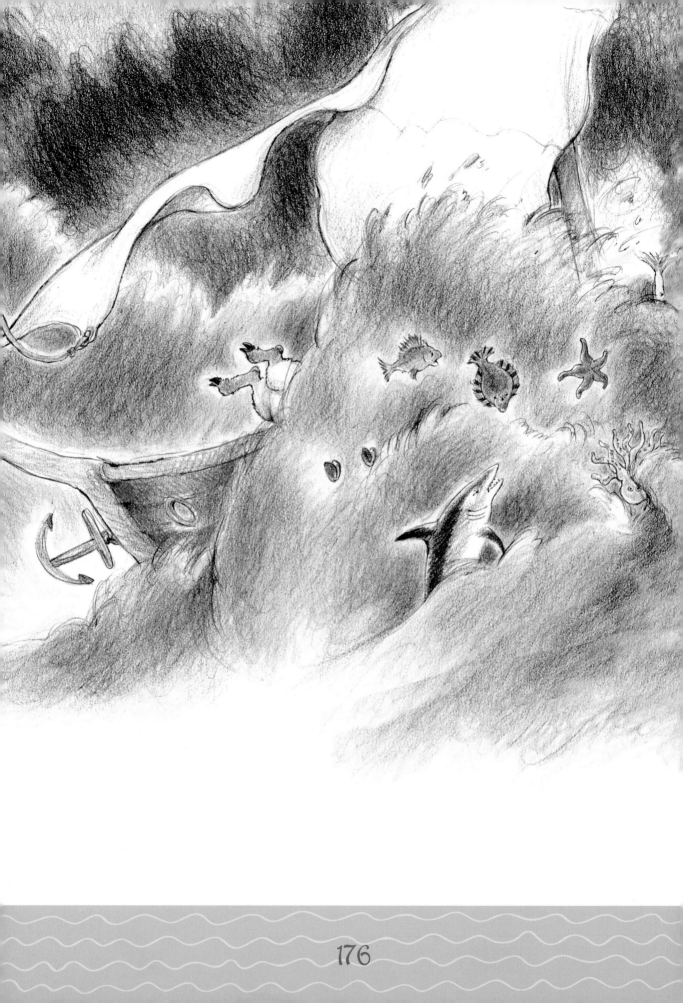

Waves wash across the ship.
Waves slosh. Sheep slip.

Decks tip.
Sheep slide.

Sheep trip.
Sheep collide.

Winds whip.
Sails rip.
Sheep can't sail
their sagging ship.

They chop a mast to make a raft.

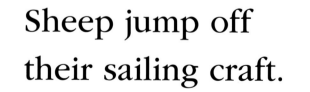

Sheep jump off
their sailing craft.

The storm lifts. The raft drifts.

Land ho!
Not far to go.

Sheep come
paddling
into port.

Sheep jump off. Sheep fall short.

Sheep climb out. Sheep drip.
Sheep are glad to end their trip.

Sheep Go to Sleep

Winking fireflies
light the way,
as sheep stroll home
to hit the hay.

Five sheep settle in their shed,
using straw to make the bed.

Screeches! Rustling! Noisy crickets!
Sheep hear hoots from nearby thickets.

Nighttime noises scare the sheep.
Really, who could go to sleep?

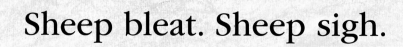

Sheep bleat. Sheep sigh.

A trusty collie wanders by.

What would make the sheep feel snug?

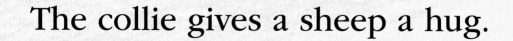

The collie gives a sheep a hug.

The tired sheep begins to snore.

One asleep! How many more?

One sheep asks to have a drink.

The collie gets it from the sink.

Another sheep begins to snore.

Two asleep! How many more?

A lullaby should calm the flock.
Sheep tap rhythm, hum, and rock.

Another sheep begins to snore.
Three asleep! How many more?

One sheep wants a teddy bear.
The collie brings his own to share.

Another sheep begins to snore.
Four asleep! How many more?

The last one wants a cozy quilt
to snuggle in the bed she built.

The collie gives a weary grin.
He fetches one and tucks her in.

All the sheep have closed their eyes.

They'll drowse and dream until sunrise.

But where is the dog
who looks after the sheep?

He's under the haystack, fast asleep.

Nancy Shaw is the author of the eight beloved tales featuring the endearing and comical sheep. She came up with the idea for the sheep books during a very long car ride with her husband and two children. She lives in Ann Arbor, Michigan, with her family. Visit her at nancyshawbooks.com.

Margot Apple is a freelance illustrator, having illustrated more than fifty books for children while also producing illustrations for *Cricket* and *Ladybug* magazines. She now lives in Shelburne Falls, Massachusetts, with her husband and their pets.

Enjoy the other 5-minute story collections: